Favor Johnson

A Christmas Story

www.bunkerhillpublishing.com
First published in 2009
by Bunker Hill Publishing Inc.
285 River Road, Piermont
New Hampshire 03779, USA

10 9 8 7 6 5 4 3 2 1

Library of Congress Control Number: 2009927978
ISBN 978-1-59373-082-6

Designed by Peter Holm, Sterling Hill Productions
Printed in China by Jade Productions

Written by
Willem Lange

Illustrated by
Bert Dodson

Snow was falling in the village on Christmas Eve. The brook rattled down behind the post office. People had finished supper. Christmas tree lights shone through their windows. The village seemed to be waiting for something.

About seven in the evening, an old blue pickup truck with shaky headlights drove slowly into the village and stopped at the first house.

A man in overalls and an old red-and-black checked jacket got out and trudged up to the kitchen door of the house with a small package wrapped in aluminum foil.

He knocked on the door. When a woman opened it, the man in overalls handed her the shiny package. Then everyone else in the house came to the door to say hello. As he walked back to his truck, they all called after him, "Merry Christmas!" and he waved.

He drove to the next house and did the same thing. Then on to the next, and all the way down through the village. After the last house, he turned his truck around, drove back through the village, and disappeared into the night. Favor Johnson had delivered his Christmas presents again.

They were fruit cakes baked in tin cans. For two people, it was a soup can. For small families, a vegetable can. For large families, a tomato can. Mixed with butter and filled with hickory nuts, cherries, pineapple, citron, and raisins, the fruit cakes were flavored with hard cider.

Favor lived on a broken-down old hill farm about two miles above the village. He was poor, and lived
there alone.

Well, not quite alone. He had an old horse, a few cows, a coop full of chickens, six geese, about forty cats, and his constant companion, a spotted hound named Hercules.

Then one year Favor's property taxes went up, and he couldn't pay them anymore. So he decided to sell his hilltop, which had a view to the west all the way to the Green Mountains.

The hilltop was bought by Doctor Jennings, a surgeon from Massachusetts. Doc Jennings and his wife had a big stone-and-glass house built, where they hoped to retire someday. They came every Friday night and went back home again Sunday evening.

Favor liked the Jenningses. They usually came down to his house Saturday mornings to talk or buy a few eggs or maple syrup. Sometimes they invited him to dinner. Favor was always polite, but he never went.

Then, one Christmas Eve, Hercules, for the first time in his life, didn't show up at the barn for the evening milking. Favor whistled and called, but there was no answer.

Then Favor remembered he'd heard rabbit hunters down in his swamp that afternoon. So, after milking, he got his flashlight and headed down the hill. It was dark and beginning to snow.

He wandered for hours through the swamp, calling and whistling.

Finally he heard a whine and found Hercules. He'd
been shot. His head and shoulder were bleeding
onto the snow. Favor scooped him up and headed
toward the house. His flashlight faded and died.

Just as Favor reached the road with Hercules
in his arms, the headlights of a car swept
across him. It was Doc and his wife,
headed for the Christmas Eve
church service. The big car
skidded to a stop, and Doc
jumped out. "What's
happened?" he cried.

Favor told him. "Well, come on!" said Doc. "Let's get him to a vet!" "Nope," said Favor. "I don't want to do that. This is the only home he's ever known. If he's gonna die, it ought to be right here." Tears and sweat ran together down his face.

"Okay," said Doc. "Honey, will you run up the hill and get the first-aid kit in the kitchen, please? Come on, Favor, let's get that dog in the house." They carried Hercules into Favor's kitchen. Doc told Favor to boil some water.

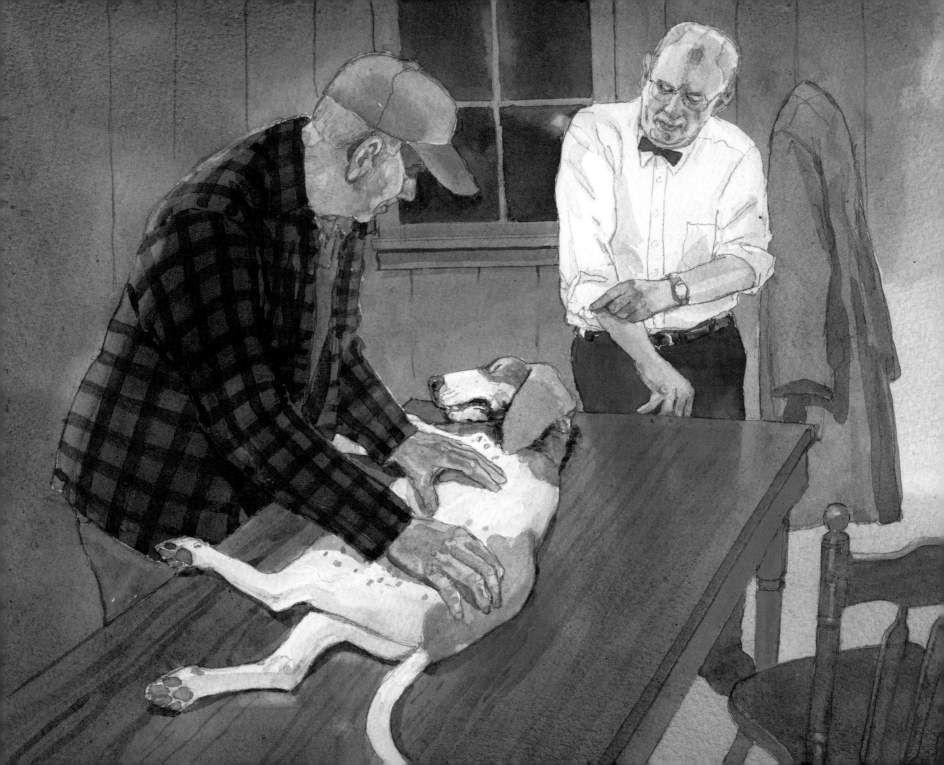

Doc took off his coat and examined Hercules. His jaw was broken. Some teeth were missing. His shoulder had been torn open. He was moaning and panting. "I don't know if it's proper to pray for a dog, Favor," said Doc. "But it can't hurt. This old guy's not in very good shape."

Mrs. Jennings brought the first-aid kit and some sweet rolls. She brewed coffee while Doc worked and Favor watched.

About three in the morning Doc took his last stitch, swabbed the wounds with antiseptic, and gave the exhausted dog a shot for the pain.

They lifted Hercules and laid him very gently on his mat beside the stove. "Thanks, Doc," said Favor. "He looks a lot better'n he did. What do I owe you?"

"Owe me?" said Doc. "Why, nothing. I know you'd do whatever you could for me if I needed it, and this was just something I could do for you. You'd better get some sleep."

When Doc came down to check on Hercules and Favor, late on Christmas morning, Hercules was too weak to raise his head. But his long tail thumped on his mat. "I think he's going to be all right," said Doc. "Merry Christmas!" He handed Favor a fancy boxed fruitcake.

Favor thanked him again for saving Hercules, and for the fruitcake. But later, tasting it, he gagged. "Pfah!" he exclaimed. "I can do better'n that!"

And that's how it started. He made just one that first year, for Doc and Mrs. Jennings. They liked it so much that the next year he made a few more for some old friends.

The response was tremendous, and within a few years he was making them for everybody in the village. And the village responded. Now, all through the Christmas season there are cars in his dooryard, and his kitchen is piled high with gifts that he enjoys all through the long winter.

Some of the village kids even think he's
Santa Claus in disguise.

That seems to give him the greatest
pleasure of all!